The Man Who Was Too Lazy to Fix Things

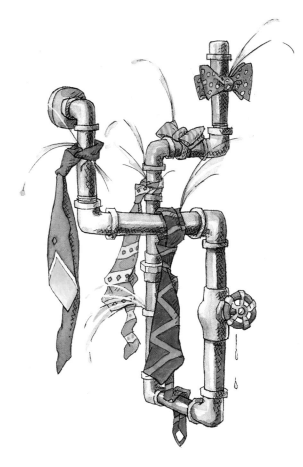

PHYLLIS KRASILOVSKY

pictures by JOHN EMIL CYMERMAN

The Man Who Was Too Lazy to Fix Things

Tambourine Books  New York

Text copyright © 1992 by Phyllis Krasilovsky
Illustrations copyright © 1992 by John Emil Cymerman

All rights reserved. No part of this book may be reproduced or
utilized in any form or by any means, electronic or mechanical,
including photocopying, recording, or by any information storage or
retrieval system, without permission in writing from the Publisher.
Inquiries should be addressed to Tambourine Books,
a division of William Morrow & Company, Inc.,
1350 Avenue of the Americas, New York, New York 10019.
Printed in Italy
The full-color illustrations were created using
pen and ink and watercolor.

Library of Congress Cataloging in Publication Data
Krasilovsky, Phyllis. The man who was too lazy to fix things/by
Phyllis Krasilovsky; pictures by John Emil Cymerman. p. cm.
Summary: A man tries to take shortcuts in making the badly needed repairs
to his aging house but finds himself in a worse situation than before.
[1. Dwellings—Maintenance and repair—Fiction.   2. Repairing—Fiction]
I. Cymerman, John Emil, ill. II. Title.
PZ7.K865Maw 1992 [E]—dc20 91-435 CIP AC
ISBN 0-688-10394-4 (trade) —ISBN 0-688-10395-2 (lib.)

1 3 5 7 9 10 8 6 4 2
First edition

For my beloved grandson, Thomas Finney

P.K.

Thank you, Mary Reiss

J.E.C.

Once there was a man who lived with his cat in a little house on the edge of town. He had no wife or children, so his life was very simple.

When the man bought the house everything was fresh and new. The paint sparkled, the windows shined, and all the furniture was in good shape. Even the trees around the house were well trimmed.

But after several years went by things began to fall apart.

At first the man didn't notice. He was too busy doing the things he enjoyed most ... rocking on his porch chair, reading,

fishing,

and cooking.

One day the man knocked over his favorite plate. He liked to eat from it because its blue flowers seemed to make the food taste better. "Oh dear, oh dear," he said.

He was too lazy to go to the store for strong glue so he mixed flour and water together and pasted the plate as best he could. Then he stood on a chair to put it on a high shelf.

Just as he stepped down, the chair broke. A rung had fallen off.

The man knew he had some wire in the cellar *somewhere*. It would take him hours to find it so he wrapped a lot of Band-Aids around the rung to hold the chair together.

The chair felt rickety and looked terrible, so he moved it to the other side of the table.

Unfortunately, he brushed against a picture on the wall. It fell with a clatter and the frame nearly broke. The picture was one he was very fond of, showing his cat wearing a big ribbon.

Instead of fetching a hammer, he used his shoe to knock the nail back into the wall. The nail went right through the sole!

The man tore off some pages from his calendar and stuffed them into his shoe.

The nail wobbled so the picture hung crookedly. "I must remember to replace that nail with a hook," he said to himself.

While he was hopping around in one shoe, the cat started to scratch against the front door, trying to get in. When the man saw that she had scratched paint off the door he was angry, but not too angry. It was simple enough for him to touch it up with shoe polish. "That will cover it until I get around to painting," he said. But he kept forgetting to do it.

It was amazing how many things suddenly needed attention! One day there was a big storm. A heavy tree branch fell on the front walk and cracked it. It made the man tired just to think of shopping for cement and mixing it up and filling in the crack. Instead, he chewed up a lot of chewing gum while he sat rocking in his chair.

When the gum was nice and soft he spread it over the crack. "It's the same color as the walk," he chuckled to himself. "No one will ever know the difference."

Then he saw that another tree branch had broken a
windowpane over his bed. He covered it up with a piece of
cardboard, telling himself he'd get a new pane of glass the
next time he went to town.

Now he was cold at night. The wind blew right through
the cardboard and he woke up with an annoying case
of sniffles.

The man cooked a hearty stew to keep himself warm. Just before it was ready, though, the handle of his big pot fell off. He was too lazy to fetch a screwdriver, so he tightened it with a dime. The dime was slippery and fell into the pot.

When the man ate the stew he almost swallowed the dime! The next day he had to cook with a smaller pot. Things kept boiling over on the stove and made a mess.

The man realized that it would soon be his birthday, but he couldn't tell what day it was without his calendar. His brother's family always came to visit him on his birthday. He thought this over while he rocked in his rocking chair on the porch.

While he was rocking, he noticed that the grass on his lawn had grown too high.

He noticed that the storm had washed away the shoe polish from his front door.

He realized he was tired of looking at the cat's picture hanging crookedly, and tired of freezing in his bed every night. He missed his old kitchen chair, and especially eating from his blue-flowered plate.

He jumped out of his rocking chair, determined to set everything right again.

But when the man charged down the path, he landed in the chewing gum by mistake. The sun had softened it and there were long threads sticking to his shoe. There was so much of it he could hardly pick up his feet. "Oh dear!" he moaned. "What a mess!"

Just then, his brother's family arrived. They helped to free him by getting most of the gum off.

"I was going to clean up before you came," he said, "but you surprised me by coming so early."

They were surprised that he was surprised. "But today's your birthday!" they said.

Then the man remembered he had stuffed the pages from his calendar into his shoe. No wonder he didn't know what day it was!

The lazy man got so busy that for once his cat could sit in his rocking chair!

He showed his nephew and niece and sister-in-law and brother how to cut the grass, hang the picture, screw on the pot handle, and wrap strong wire around the broken chair.

They went to town and bought cement, paint, glue, a sheet of glass, lemons, sugar, steaks, vegetables, and a special surprise.

They mixed cement, fixed the crack in the walk, and wrote everyone's initials in a big cement heart.

They painted and patched and cleaned and cooked.

Finally, they were all finished.
Everyone sat on the porch and drank
lemonade. The man went straight to
his rocking chair. He was absolutely
exhausted from showing everyone else
what to do.

The man was very happy because everything looked as good as new. Later, even his blue-flowered plate looked new, holding the special surprise his niece had bought. It was a birthday cake shaped like a house. On one side the windows were broken. On the other side they were perfect. There was a candle instead of a chimney.

Before he blew out the candle, the man closed his eyes and wished that nothing in his real house would ever break again.